THE ORCHARD BOOK OF

Ghostly Stories

by Martin Waddell

illustrated by Sophy Williams

 ORCHARD BOOKS

For Liz Weir, Herself
MW

For Oscar
SW

ORCHARD BOOKS
96 Leonard Street, London EC2A 4XD
Orchard Books Australia
14 Mars Road, Lane Cove, NSW 2066
First published in Great Britain in 2000
ISBN 1 86039 421 3
Text © Martin Waddell 2000
Illustrations © Sophy Williams 2000
The rights of Martin Waddell to be identified as the author and
Sophy Williams to be identified as the illustrator of this work
have been asserted by them in accordance with the
Copyright, Designs and Patents Act, 1988.
A CIP catalogue record for this book is available from the British Library
1 3 5 7 9 10 8 6 4 2
Printed in Hong Kong/China

Contents

Foreword

I wrote most of these ghostly stories over the course of a cold winter when I stayed in an old farmhouse along the Drumnaquoile Road, close to the Dromara Hills, in County Down.

The Drumnaquoile Road is the right place to be thinking about ghosts and the supernatural, for when darkness falls out there it is real darkness, no street lights, and there are echoes and creaks and whispers in the night which remind you that the place was there before you, and will be there long after you have gone. I've tried to catch that Irish feeling in the stories: the remoteness of the Drumnaquoile house; the dampness of the stone walls; the bleakness of a wet Irish winter, and also the country tradition of the wink and the nod, for most of these stories are tall stories . . . You don't have to believe all you are told, but it could be worth your while listening, for some things that are hidden inside might be worth understanding.

The first ghostly story I wrote was *Himself*. Himself is not a ghost-from-the-grave ghost, bloodless bones and sightless eye-sockets, the stuff of nightmares, but a ghost of quite another kind, a ghost from within, a ghost that everyone born has to live with. I don't know

how I came to write that story. It is like nothing I have written before and it just came. The others range from the highly mannered but raw blood-and-bone horror of *The Hunger* through the gentleness of *The Ghostly Penny* and *The Haunting at Soft Butter's Farm* to the burlesque graveyard humour of *Death and the Neighbours at Ness*. Of the eight stories, *Little Bridget* is the odd one out, for it springs directly from William Allingham's poem *The Fairies*. With *Little Bridget* I broke all my own rules about writing totally original stories, because she came into my head all-in-one-piece and the story wanted to be written. They were my rules anyway, so why not? The other stories are meant to sound and feel like old, traditional retellings, but they are my own work, freshly minted.

I enjoyed the long winter nights along the Drumnaquoile Road when I worked on these stories. I hope you will enjoy reading them.

Martin Waddell

Boneless and the Tinker

It's a lonely old Boneless, is Boneless.

It is, for It lives all alone at Bannerman's Farm, way up by the edge of the bog. Some say that Boneless was Bannerman's cow, and some say It was Bannerman's horse, or a sheep, or Bannerman's grannie that Bannerman killed and bricked up in the wall so he could steal all her money. Some say that, but no one knows, for no one goes to Bannerman's Farm, and no one has seen It, for there isn't a *shape* to old Boneless.

When Bannerman died, Boneless It cried, and Its weeping and wailing was heard on the bog. It frightened the folk who went by on the road, so they stayed away from the farm. That left Boneless to live there alone on the place.

Weeds grew in the yard, and the gate at the bend was rotting and lay in the ditch when young Kit went by, with his Ellen, his red-headed wife, and his child and their cart. Young Kit, footsore, was dragging the cart on the bog track, for he hadn't the price of the beast that could pull it. Kit pulled it along, for Ellen was his wife and the love of his life and he wanted to find her a home.

"There's a fine place," said Ellen, trudging along at the back of their cart, with their child on her back.

"Well, I'd say so!" said Kit, and he stopped pulling the cart and stepped out of the shafts.

"We're beggars with no place to go," Ellen said, "so we'll not be too choosy!"

"You're right there, my Ellen," said Kit.

He pushed by the gate and trudged up the lane for a look at the place, for he didn't know it was Bannerman's Farm, with Bannerman gone.

Kit beat on the door, but no one answered, for no one was there but Boneless, and Boneless don't answer the knocks on Its door.

Kit broke the door in, and wandered inside for a minute, then he came skipping out with a shout, and he called down the lane for his wife and child.

Ellen hitched up her skirt and tightened her grip on the child on her back, and she ran up the lane, to see what had become of her Kit. She thought he was hurt from the howl that he gave; but he wasn't hurt.

Kit was dancing about, like a clown.

"See here, Ellen dear!" shouted Kit. "Here's a grand house we can turn to a home, for yourself and myself and the child."

He showed Ellen into the house.

Ellen looked round in amazement.

Though the windows were cracked and the roof was in holes and the water had run down the walls, the floor was as clean as a whistle and there were the tables and chairs and a bed and a hob made of brass by the fire, all shined up and glowy and neat.

It was Boneless did that, but they didn't know it, for they'd never heard tell of old Boneless.

"Well I declare!" Ellen said. "Here we are on the pig's back!"

Kit was as pleased as Punch, as well he might be, for he was a man with a wife and a child and no home, and all of a sudden he'd found one, sitting empty . . . so it seemed, though the place wasn't empty at all. The old house was filled with old Boneless.

The young pair soon got busy, fixing the roof and mending the gate, and cutting the weeds that grew in the yard, and they soon had the place like a farm again, with seed planted out in the field. Kit was helped by Boneless, though he never knew that. Whatever Kit did, Boneless did more, ditching and thatching and mending the fences. Boneless did his share, for he liked having them there. It was lonely, was Boneless. It liked having young life round the place.

That was all right, till the handsome Tinker came meddling! He should have stuck to his pots and his pans and never let out with his talking, but that wasn't the way with the Tinker, for the Tinker was mean and he lived by taking his chances.

The Tinker came by one day, when Kit was out on the bog cutting turf, and he saw the lane cleared and the gate back on its post, so he turned up the lane to Bannerman's Farm.

There was pretty young Ellen out by the byre, with the sun shining down on her fiery red hair.

"You'll likely be needing my new pots and pans?" the Tinker said.

"I likely will not!" Ellen said, for she hadn't two pennies to rub together.

"Where's your man?" said the Tinker, for the Tinker was cunning and cautious.

"He's away in the bog," Ellen said. "And what's that to you?"

"I was thinking; a pot for a kiss?" the Tinker said, with a wink.

"You're out of your mind!" Ellen said, tossing her head and blushing bright red.

"Two pots and a pan?" said the Tinker.

Two pots and a pan would make a good dinner for Kit, and she was Kit's wife and she wanted to please him.

She put out her hand and she felt the cold iron of the pan.

"Sure, what's in a kiss?" said the Tinker, seeing the look on her face.

No harm at all! thought young Ellen. So she gave the bold Tinker a kiss, and she got two pots and a pan, the best in his pack, from the Tinker.

Ellen knew that her Kit would be mad at her kissing the Tinker, so she hid the two pots and the pan in the dresser so no one would know they were there – no one but Boneless, but she didn't know It was about.

That night Boneless was out in the kitchen, shaking and rattling Itself, and rocking the dresser.

It spilled the new pots and the pan on the floor, as though It was trying to bust them.

"What's this about, wife?" Kit asked, when he'd come down and looked at the kitchen. There was a bent pan on the floor, and two pots with their handles all twisted and broken.

"I'm sure I don't know," answered Ellen, and neither she did, for she'd never heard of old Boneless. Just the same, she told herself not to talk to the Tinker again, for something seemed sad in the house.

Next week Kit went to the fair, and when he went off down the lane the Tinker came out of the blueberry bush where he'd hidden, for the Tinker was careful and cautious, and he knew he was no match for Kit.

The bold Tinker whistled his way up the lane. In the pack on his back he had fine lace that he'd stolen, for he was a thief as well as a tinker.

Ellen barred the door, but he knocked on the window, and showed her the lace through the pane.

It was beautiful lace. She thought she could wear it for Kit, for he loved to see her look grand, though her dresses were old, and she was Kit's wife and she wanted to please him.

So the Tinker got into the house.

Would she give him his kiss?

He went away with a smile on his face, and no lace!

That night by the fire, Ellen sat stitching fine lace on her dress but then . . .

The door opened and banged.

And a wind blew on the fire so the flames flew out in her face, and burned the fine lace she was stitching.

It was Boneless again, but she didn't know that.

Well, maybe she did, for she buried the burned dress with the lace at the back of the byre, where no one would see it, and she vowed to herself not to talk any more to the Tinker, no matter what fine thing he'd bring her.

The next time Kit went down the lane, Ellen ran over the field, and she called him back. They walked up the field to the house and Ellen told Kit that she needed him home, for she didn't like being alone. It was true, for by now Ellen was scared that she'd talk to the Tinker again, and then things would go wrong in the house. Kit did as she asked, for she was his wife and the love of his life.

The Tinker popped out of the blueberry bush and whistled his way up the lane, but Ellen had Kit by her side, and he chased the bold Tinker away down the lane, with a flea in his ear!

They were happy that night in the firelight and somehow, I think, so was Boneless.

But that wasn't the end of the Tinker.

The Tinker was crafty and bided his time. When next Kit went off, the Tinker was there to watch him go past, hid in the blueberry bush. When Kit had gone on the Tinker came out, and whistled his way up the lane.

"Get off our land, Tinker!" said Ellen.

"Look what I have here," said the Tinker.

The Tinker showed Ellen bright gold, that glittered and shone like moon-yellow. The Tinker was crafty and cute and a cheat, for it was fool's gold and he'd made it himself at the fire in the wood.

"I'll tell my Kit," Ellen said, tossing her head.

"See how it shines!" said the Tinker, and he gave her the gold to hold in her hand.

Ellen looked at the gold. It shone in her hand like the moon, and she wanted it badly, for she thought she could string the bright gold in her hair, and she'd seem lovely to Kit, for she was his wife and she wanted to please him.

"Just one kiss?" said the Tinker.

Ellen gave in, and she took his fool's gold.

The Tinker went off with a spring in his step, and Ellen was left with her gold.

Ellen looked at the bright gold in her hand, and she thought about Kit. They were poor. How could she tell him she'd got it?

She didn't know how, so she hid the gold under the stair. No one would know it was there – no one but Boneless, but poor Ellen didn't know that.

If she didn't, she knew it that night.

All was quiet and still as they sat by the fire, but suddenly It was about.

Boneless blew down the chimney, scattering the fire. It roared round the room and It shook the old stair. The wood shattered and broke, and the next thing they knew It had chucked the fool's gold all over Ellen.

"What's this, my Ellen?" said Kit,
as he looked at the gold.
"I don't know at all,"
Ellen lied.
That was too much
for Boneless.
It picked Ellen up, and It
took her and tore all her
clothes and shoved her
about in the room and tossed
her and turfed her right out of
the house. Then It blew Ellen
tree-high down the lane, and threw
her away in the blueberry bush where
the Tinker had hid from young Kit.
Poor Kit was heart-scared. He ran to
their room and picked up their child,
and he tore down the lane to his wife,
for she was the love of his life.
That was the end of Bannerman's
Farm for the pair. Boneless
hadn't counted on that. But
Ellen was scared, so was Kit,
so they went off over the bog
with their cart, and they
never came back to
Bannerman's Farm.

It wasn't too bad for Ellen and Kit and their child. They lost their farm, but Ellen loved Kit and she wanted to please him, and she was the love of his life. No doubt they got on very well in the end, as some lovers do.

It doesn't know much about love, doesn't Boneless, but It knows about being alone, and Boneless knew who was to blame.

Boneless was there at Bannerman's Farm, filled with cold hate for the Tinker.

And the bold Tinker came.

He whistled his way up the lane to the sweetheart he thought he had stolen from Kit.

Boneless was there in her place, and Boneless was waiting.

No one knows what became of the Tinker.

No one has seen his cold bones lying at Bannerman's Farm, out there along the bog track.

No one knows they are there, but old Boneless.

It's a lonely old Boneless, is Boneless.

Death and the Neighbours at Ness

Old Nagger Barr keeps her farm next door to the graveyard at Ness. The lane past her door is the corpse path, where coffins bump by on the shoulders of men; it is the way to the grave for herself, and the neighbours.

One time, a long time ago, Nagger's young grandson arrived on the farm. His name was Fintan McGlone. Nagger was old even then, and Fintan had come to the farm in the hope he'd inherit when she died. Nagger Barr gave him his orders about how to do the different jobs on the farm, but he was lazy and he shirked the work. He made Nagger mad. She scolded and moaned and she chased him all day round the farm, though it didn't do her much good.

One day Nagger felt poorly, and so she called to the boy to come into the house.

"The way you go on, who's to care for the farm when I'm gone to the neighbours?" groaned old Nagger.

"What neighbours?" asked Fintan McGlone.

"The neighbours above that rest in their graves," said old Nagger. "I'm feared for the farm, once you get your hands on it,

for you are no farmer."

"I'll do the job fine," Fintan said, thinking of how he would spend all the money that she'd kept hidden in jam jars all over her house.

"Well, mind that you do," scolded Nagger. "If you don't mend your ways and take care of my farm when I'm gone, I'll come back!"

Fintan grinned to himself. When you're dead, you stay dead. She couldn't come back, and she knew it, for all of her nagging. The nagging would stop when Nagger was brought to the grave . . . then Fintan would have his reward, for he'd have her good farm.

Soon after that old Nagger died, still groaning and moaning about whether Fintan would care for her farm, and keep things the way they should be.

Fintan had the wake for her that night along with his friends. Old Nagger was there, all dolled up in lace, sat up in her coffin. It was laid out on a plank and some chairs in the kitchen, after the way at a wake.

"You'll never come back," Fintan laughed down at old Nagger Barr in her box. "You're dead and gone. From now on, I'm having this farm," and he danced around her with his friends.

Old Nagger Barr didn't stir. Death had her, and Death wasn't giving her back . . . or so Fintan thought.

Next day Fintan and his friends nailed the lid down and they carried old Nagger along the corpse path to the graveyard at Ness. The priest said the prayers and they buried old Nagger way down in the earth. Then they went back to the house and they all ate and drank a bit more. After that, the others went back to their houses, and left Fintan alone, drinking and searching the place for old Nagger's jars full of money. He was up to all hours till he found them, with never a thought for the farm, or the beasts.

The night wore on, and Fintan went to sleep by the fire in Nagger's old chair, with a glass in his hand, and her jam jars around him, all filled with her money, well pleased now her money was his. He went to sleep. He dreamed of how much he would spend and how he would sell up the farm, and open a bar called The House of McGlone, full of hard drink that he'd sell to his friends. The best joke of it was that her money would pay for the bar, which would really have soured poor old Nagger, who never let drink pass her lips.

Bang! came a knock at the door, and that woke Fintan up. It was a knock that would waken the dead, if Death let them wake, which Death wouldn't . . . or so Fintan thought.

"Who's that at this hour?" called Fintan McGlone from his seat by the fire.

"O'Riordan, your neighbour," a voice answered back from outside the door.

"The only O'Riordan I know is called Dan, and he died this yesteryear!" said Fintan McGlone.

"That's me," said the voice, greatly astonishing Fintan McGlone. He ran to the door and he pulled it wide open, thinking some of his friends had come to play a joke on him, after the death of old Nagger Barr.

Dan O'Riordan was there, large as life, but in death, for he wore his grave-clothes and he looked a bit gone, as well he might, having been dead for a year.

"Goodnight to you, Fintan," said O'Riordan. "I'm not coming in. I just called down to say that we're having trouble up there with old Nagger Barr. She's out of her box, and drifting around moaning about what you've been doing down here. She's nagging us all, and complaining, and we're getting no sleep in our graves."

"What ails the woman?" asked Fintan McGlone. "Isn't she dead? Why won't she lie down like her neighbours?"

"She's mad at you for not minding the cow," said O'Riordan. "It's out in the field and it's never been milked today, while you were in here drinking beer with your friends and counting her money. She says I'm to tell you, if you don't mend your ways, she'll come back to her farm."

"By jings, I forgot the old cow!" said Fintan. "I'll deal with the cow, and you can tell that to old Nagger, like the good neighbour you are. Tell her to mind she stays put where she is with the neighbours up there in the grave, for Death's put a stop to her nagging of me, and this farm is Fintan McGlone's. It doesn't belong to old Nagger Barr any more, for she's dead."

Fintan dealt
with the cow, and
O'Riordan went back
to the graveyard above, but
who knows what he said to old
Nagger, or just how he put it.

That was all that happened that night,
but the very next night, as young Fintan sat
down to his meal, there came a *Bang! Bang!* at the
door, so loud that he choked on his food. He sprang
up from the table, and he almost broke
the fine china he'd bought for himself that day at the
shops, when he went down to spend old Nagger's money.

"Who's that at my door?" called Fintan McGlone.

"Your neighbour, Soraghan!" answered a voice.

"Are you the Soraghan that's been dead these
long years?" said Fintan, for he thought it might be,
considering what happened the evening before.

"That's right," said a voice. "Soraghan from

out of the grave. I came down to say that your Nagger's making an awful fuss. She said to say you've not put the hens in, and you're spending her money on stuff that just isn't fit for a farmer. And we wouldn't mind that, but she's shouting at us, not at you, and we are too dead to look after your hens."

"The hens are all right where they are," said Fintan, opening the door to look at Soraghan, to check out that it was dead Soraghan that was there, for he didn't sort much with the Soraghan clan. If this one was alive, then Fintan would give him a kicking and send him away. Soraghan was there in his grave shroud, just a bit bony and thin, and grey round the eyes. He'd gone quite a bit. Fintan could see the wall through him, so there was nothing worth kicking to kick.

"Now listen here, Fintan McGlone," said dead Soraghan. "You know and I know the hens are all right where they are, but old Nagger says that they're not, and she's scaring the neighbours above with her moaning and groaning. If you don't shape up, she swears she'll come back to her farm. Better put the hens in, and lay her to rest, or you'll have all of us down the lane haunting your house. Haunting you won't be easy for us, considering how long we've been dead, and Death doesn't like haunters one bit. But we'd do it just to be free of her nagging."

"I'm not scared of you graveyard people," said Fintan McGlone. "I can take care of an old pack of ghosts, and this farm is mine now. It has nothing to do with old Nagger."

"If you think so," said Soraghan, "it just goes to show that you don't know your Nagger."

The dead man was so cross he was grinding his teeth, which was a bit odd, considering how he had no teeth left to grind. The dead are like that. They do things for show when they're haunting.

The end of it was Fintan got the hens in, and Soraghan went back to his grave, while Fintan was counting the eggs.

The next night, Fintan was watching TV on a new set that he'd bought with the egg-money. There'd been a man up from the town to install it, and now Fintan was watching a horse race, with the form book spread out on his knee.

Bang! Bang! Bang! went the door.

"Come in," shouted Fintan McGlone, knowing who it would be: some dead neighbour's ghost come down from the graveyard with more complaints from old Nagger Barr and more of her threats that she'd come back and haunt him.

"Are you asking me in?" said a voice.

"Didn't I say so?" said Fintan McGlone. "Just wipe your bones on the mat, for that dust from the grave is awful messy, and I have had my new carpet fitted and laid, now I've got my hands on the money."

The door opened and in came a huge man all covered up in a black cloak and a hood, with a sack on his back. He laid the sack on Fintan's new blue carpet and he stood himself up by the fire. He was so big that he blocked the TV and Fintan missed the end of the race.

"Well, you're welcome here on my farm," said Fintan McGlone, running his mind down the list of the dead to think who this one might be, for he didn't look like one of the neighbours above in the graveyard, or not one that Fintan could recognise.

"It's not often I'm asked to come in," said the man.

Fintan thought a bit more, but he still couldn't put a name to the stranger before him. At last he said, "I'm ashamed to admit it, but though I'm sure I knew you well when you were alive,

just now I can't put a name
to your face."

"My name is Death," said
the man, and he pulled
down his hood and opened
his cloak, so Fintan could
see who he was.

All that Death had was
dry bones, and no flesh at all,
no eyes, no nose, no nails on
his fingers and toes, though
he'd rotting black teeth that
he showed as he grinned at
Fintan and spoke. "I called in
to leave you this sack."

"What's in the sack?"
asked Fintan McGlone, a
little bit alarmed to think
he was talking to Death.
Death belonged with the
neighbours who slept
in the graveyard
next door, and
didn't belong in
the house.

"I've brought Nagger back," said Death, and he tumbled the old woman out on the floor from the sack. "She doesn't like your ways so she's scolding and moaning and groaning about, and spoiling the peace of the grave for the others, and all on account of your wrecking her farm, and spending her money like water. It's all your fault. That's why you're getting her back, because the neighbours up there can't abide her." Then Death twirled his cloak and swirled up the chimney and vanished.

Fintan looked down at old Nagger, who still seemed very dead as she lay on the new carpet he'd put on the floor. She stirred a bit, and her eyes opened wide, and she grinned up at Fintan, delighted.

"I said I'd come back to my farm," she told Fintan. "I'm back, alive, and I'm staying, and bad cess to you, young McGlone!"

They're both there to this day on the farm, on the corpse path to the graveyard at Ness. Old Nagger Barr won't leave her farm till Fintan McGlone has mended his ways, and Fintan's still hoping she'll drop down and leave him her money one day and so . . . Fintan's waiting for Death to come to the door, but Death won't be calling for Nagger just yet . . .

Death's not letting her back in the graveyard at Ness, he's not letting her back, for she was upsetting the neighbours, poor souls.

Gallows Hill

One night Sam Bonny was coming home on the old donkey he had bought at the fair with the money he got for selling his eggs. He had stayed on at the fair after buying the donkey, and so it was dusk when he came to the crossroad at Strule, on his way to his house on the slopes of Slieve Crobe, in the townland of Menagh.

As everyone knows, there are two roads that go from Strule on to Menagh.

One road leads by the black bog into Menagh. It is the long road, and it's muddy. The short road is the road by the hill with the gallows. No one goes by that road in the dark, but that night Sam Bonny did.

He wanted to get to his home before dawn, and Strule is a long way from Menagh if you take the bog road, but no distance at all if you go by the hill. There was always some poor body hung out on the hill.

As everyone knows, men don't take that road because of the corpses that hang out on the hill.

"Well, so there it is!" Sam told himself. "But what corpse would

be bothering me? If I go by the hill I'll be home before dawn, and if I go by the Bog I'll be covered in mud and home late."

He'd a day's work to do on the farm the next day, and so he set off on the road to the hill.

He had no bother till he came to the Gallows.

His neighbour Jackie Golightly swung there, strung up and choked for poaching a salmon belonging to the magistrate, Big Lord McGill.

As everyone knows, Big Lord McGill is a keen fisherman, and likes to catch his own salmon.

Everyone knew, and Jackie Golightly didn't mean to be caught, but he was, and so he was sentenced and hanged, for the salmon.

The donkey stopped there, at the gallows, and it laid its ears back and brayed, looking up at the corpse of Jackie Golightly.

"God rest your soul!" Sam said. He crossed himself thrice, to ward off the curse, and he tipped his hat to the corpse, for there's no harm in being polite. "It's a hard thing to be hanged for eating a fish."

Everyone knows Sam didn't eat fish, except on a Friday, when his wife made him eat fish and like it.

Then Sam tapped the donkey to make it go on.

The donkey wouldn't move!

That's when Sam remembered why the donkey had been cheap at the fair. It had belonged to Jackie Golightly before he was hanged! Jackie's things had been sold at the fair to pay up the debts that he owed, and repay Big Lord McGill for his salmon.

"You belong to me now," he told the donkey. "For you are no use to Jackie Golightly, up there."

The donkey wouldn't see sense.

Sam got off and pulled, but the donkey pulled back. It wasn't leaving Jackie Golightly.

Sam sat down and thought at the foot of the gallows, with Jackie Golightly swinging above him.

"If the moke won't go on, maybe it will go back," Sam thought, so he pulled the donkey the other way, back down the way leading to Strule.

The donkey stuck its hoofs in and stayed where it was, under the legs of Jackie Golightly.

"You won't come, you won't go!" Sam scolded the donkey.

The donkey stood placid and still. It was waiting for Jackie Golightly to tell it to come or to go.

"We're not staying here," Sam told the donkey. "I paid my good egg-money so I could ride, and we're not staying here on this hill."

The donkey sat down. It wouldn't go without Jackie Golightly. It wouldn't go, and Sam wouldn't leave it, but somehow he had to get home before dawn, and with him he wanted the donkey to prove how he'd spent the egg-money. His wife was the kind who might say he had spent the egg-money on drink if he went home, leaving the donkey behind.

"Talk sense, donkey dear," Sam said to the donkey.

As everyone knows, there's no talking sense to a donkey.

There was only one thing to be done, and Sam did it, for he wasn't leaving his newly-bought donkey for Jackie Golightly to keep.

He got out his knife, and he climbed up the gallows and cut down the corpse of Jackie Golightly.

"We'll take Jackie with us," Sam told the donkey, and he loaded Jackie up on its back.

That pleased the donkey.

As everyone knows, a donkey is easily pleased when it has its own way.

It pleased the donkey, but it didn't please Sam because Jackie Golightly was riding the beast, and Sam was left walking beside them, trying to hold Jackie's corpse in its place. Jackie Golightly kept slipping and sliding about on the back of the beast, for Jackie was dead and he couldn't hang on to the donkey.

"There's room for one more on your back," Sam told the donkey and he climbed up behind Jackie Golightly, wrapping his arm round the corpse to hold it on as they rode.

They went down Gallows Hill, the donkey, and Sam, and the dead man, jogging along at the slow pace of the donkey.

Sam was pleased with himself for solving the problem.

"Never mind, Jackie," said Sam. "This is better than walking!"

If the corpse nodded its head, it must have been that its poor neck was broken.

As everyone knows, no corpse can go nodding its head, especially a corpse that's been dead for a week, and hung out in the cold.

The trouble started halfway to Menagh, and halfway to Sam's home. They were drawing close to the lane leading up to the house that belonged to Jackie Golightly, before he was hanged.

Sam had his hand on the rein that he'd rigged, an old bit of rope that he used for a belt for his trousers. He'd brought no rein with him when he went to the fair, for he hadn't thought he'd be coming home with a donkey. Donkeys came dear, but this one

had come cheap, because it had belonged to Jackie Golightly.

As everyone knows, a dead man's donkey doesn't bring luck with the stripe on its back, and there hadn't been many bidders.

Sam had his hand on the rope, holding it loose, for the donkey knew the road well. He'd been down it before, with Jackie Golightly.

Sam had one hand round the waist of the corpse that was riding before him, and one hand on the rope.

Then the corpse moved.

It put out its hand, and tugged on the rope, at least Sam thought it did (although Sam knew it couldn't). And the donkey thought it did too. At least that's how Sam explains why the donkey turned up the lane at Golightly's.

"Whoa there, donkey!" cried Sam, but the donkey went on up the lane, making light of the weight on its back, that was Jackie Golightly, and Sam.

They rode into the yard at Golightly's.

The donkey came to a stop by the door, for it knew its journey was done, and it wanted a bag and some feed.

As everyone knows, a donkey deserves its desserts.

"Well, this is a to-do!" muttered Sam.

The corpse nodded again, or Sam thought it did.

Sam cursed the donkey, and got off its back.

The corpse climbed off too, all by itself.

"Back home again!" said the corpse, with a sigh, rubbing its hand on the weals round its neck.

As everyone knows, corpses don't sigh when they've been dead a week, but this corpse did, greatly upsetting poor Sam.

"You'd best be on your way," said the corpse. "For this is my home and your home's over there, Sammy Bonny."

Sam was upset, but he wasn't leaving the donkey he'd bought fair and square at the fair, at the cost of his hard-earned egg-money.

"It may be your home," Sam said, "but the donkey is mine, for I bid a fair price at the fair!"

"You bought a cheap ride that would carry you home," said the corpse. "Now you've had a ride that was worth every penny you paid. You've had your ride, Sammy, and I'm having my donkey!"

"The donkey is mine!" Sam said, standing up for his rights, although he was quaking inside. "This donkey is mine, 'cause you're dead."

"Dead I may be," said the corpse. "But I'm not staying here. I'm moving along on my donkey, in case they might swing me again on the gallows. For Gallows Hill is a cold place, and lonely, when you're hanging about and can't even hear your heart beat."

"I'm sorry you're dead," Sam said. "But I paid my egg-money, and I need the cash, or the donkey."

That seemed to make the corpse mad.

"What's your egg-money to me now I'm dead?" said the corpse, and it reached out for Sam and fixed its cold hands round Sam's throat.

That was too much for Sam Bonny.

The corpse wasn't strong (it had, after all, been dead for a week, and was just a bit into decay) so Sam shook it off, and he ran down the lane and away up the road.

That's how Sam explained coming home from the fair with no donkey to show for his money.

"It's lies! You spent our egg-money on drink!" Sam's wife cried, and she didn't feed him for a week.

Everyone knew she was right.

Everyone knew . . . but . . .

Why was there no corpse on the gallows next day? Corpses don't just ride away, and everyone knows Jackie Golightly was deader than dead for a week, stiff as a board and well into decay.

Well, everyone knew, but the donkey.

The Ghostly Penny

This story is as much about a place as it is about people, for people are made by the places they live in, like the cold lonely mountain at Creevy.

Abe and Marty Quinn lived there. They were brothers, but they had a grudge between them over a penny they'd lost, when their mother had sent them for milk a long time ago.

They lived on and grew old, up the same lane on the same mountain, but in two separate houses living alone, and all for the sake of a greasy old penny for milk.

One day Abe took a cold in the chest, and the next day he was dead.

If Marty was sad that his brother had died, he didn't show it.

He went to the graveside when his brother was buried, and spoke never a word. He dropped the last sod on the lid of the coffin, then he went to wait for the bus to go home.

Abe's ghost was waiting for him at the bus stop, and it had a strange look on its face, as though it was fretting.

The Ghost didn't speak, but neither did Marty.

The old man and the Ghost sat on the window-ledge of Higgins' Shoe Shop, waiting for the bus to come round the Square.

The bus came, and Marty got on.

"I was sorry to hear about your brother," the driver said to Marty.

"There was no love lost between us," Marty said.

He didn't care if the Ghost heard him.

The Ghost got on the bus after Marty, but the driver didn't speak to him or punch his ticket. It was as if the Ghost wasn't there.

The Ghost came down the aisle of the bus, and sat in the seat behind his brother.

There were two young girls sitting opposite the Ghost, but they didn't see him.

There's only me can see him! Marty thought.

Marty got off at the crossroads.

So did the Ghost.

They both walked down the road to the Mass rock, and then they turned up the lane towards the Hunger fields, and the two cottages a mile apart on the side of the mountain.

They started up the lane, but not together.

Marty was in front, with the Ghost behind him.

It was getting dark, and the lane was still and full of shadows.

"Marty?" said the Ghost suddenly.

Marty ignored him.

"Marty?" called the Ghost a second time.

Marty stopped.

The Ghost came up beside him.

"I don't know what it is, Marty," the Ghost said. "But I feel a bit odd."

Marty said nothing. Abe being a ghost made no difference to Marty. Why should it?

The two of them, the old man and his brother's ghost, walked on up the lane without saying anything.

"Marty?" said the Ghost.

"Did you speak to me?" Marty said.

"I did," said the Ghost.

"Mind it was you who spoke first!" Marty said.

"I've something for you," said the Ghost, and he held out a penny.

Marty looked at the penny in the Ghost's hand. It looked a bit *ghostly*, and not like the kind he could cash.

"Keep your money!" he said. "It's no use to me now."

"I'm saying that I got it wrong," said the Ghost.

"If you're saying that, what are you *after*?" said Marty. He thought there must be a catch for Abe to give in just like that.

"Maybe you'd let me come indoors a minute?" suggested the Ghost.

"It would be the first time in fifty years!" said Marty.

"It would," said the Ghost.

"Well, come in if you have to," said Marty.

Marty went into the cottage, and the Ghost came after him. The Ghost settled in their father's old chair by the fire, where Abe used to sit before they had the quarrel.

Marty lit the oil lamp, and stirred up the fire. He threw another sod of turf on, and the glow of the flames sent a shadow dancing round the room.

Marty's shadow, that is.

The Ghost cast no shadow, although he looked solid enough.

Marty lit his pipe, and the Ghost lit his pipe.

The pair of them sat there in the firelight, and neither of them said a word.

The only sound was the ticking of their mother's wall clock.

Tick-tock, tick-tock.

A long time went by.

"You never got the electric put in?" the Ghost asked.

"I did not," said Marty.

"Me neither," said the Ghost.

They sat on, puffing their pipes and not looking at each other.

They were both used to being alone. Neither of them knew what to do when it came to having company round the fire at night.

Tick-tock, tick-tock, went the clock on the wall.

"You'll be going to your bed soon," the Ghost said at last.

"There's no hurry," Marty said.

"I should be going on up the lane to my own house," the Ghost said.

Marty didn't say anything. He just sat there puffing his pipe.

The Ghost coughed and tapped his pipe against the fire and began to fidget a little bit, as if there was something on his mind.

Marty let him fidget.

"Would you mind me asking you something, Marty?" the Ghost said, clearing his throat awkwardly to say it.

"Ask on," said Marty.

"Well, I will," said the Ghost. "I was wondering, would I be, could I be . . . ?" And he stopped, as if there was something he couldn't bring himself to say.

"Dead?" said Marty.

"Yes," said the Ghost. "That's it. Could I be dead and not know it?"

"I'd never have let you in here if you were living!" Marty said, remembering it was the brother he'd quarrelled with that he was talking to.

"I thought I was dead, only I didn't know for sure," the Ghost said.

"Well, you know now," said Marty.

They sat a bit more.

Marty put some more turf on the fire, for the glow was getting dim.

Tick-tock, tick-tock, went their mother's old clock.

"Marty?" said the Ghost.

"Yes?" said Marty.

"Marty, is there . . . is there a bit less of me than there was?"

Marty peered at the Ghost. He could see the shape of the chair through the shape of his brother.

"You're a bit faded, maybe," he said.

"Oh dear," said the Ghost.

"It would be being dead that does it," said Marty. "You're fading away."

They sat a while longer.

Tick-tock, tick-tock.

"Am I still fading?" the Ghost asked.

"A bit more than you were before," Marty said.

"I'll soon be all gone then," the Ghost said.

"I suppose so, Abe," said Marty.

"You'll be wanting to go to bed," said the Ghost.

"There's no hurry," Marty said.

The fire burned low, and at last the oil lamp started to flicker, and went out.

Tick-tock, tick-tock.

"Are you there, Abe?" Marty asked.

"Aye," said the Ghost, though his voice sounded further away.

"I see you are," said Marty, peering at the figure sitting opposite him, which was now little more than a shadow in the chair.

"I'll be gone altogether, soon," said the Ghost.

"I think you will," Marty agreed.

"You are good, keeping me company, considering we never talked much all these years," said the Ghost.

"Yes," said Marty. "All over nothing, too."

"So it was," said the Ghost. "All over nothing at all."

Tick-tock, tick-tock.

They sat on. The fire burned lower and lower, down to the last few embers that glowed in the hearth.

"Abe?" said Marty.

Tick-tock, tick-tock.

"Are you still there, Abe?"

Tick-tock, tick-tock.

Marty peered at the chair across the fire from him.

It was empty. Nothing. Not even the ghostly old penny.

"Ah well," said Marty.

Tick-tock, tick-tock.

Marty stood up, knocked his pipe against the mantel, and went to bed. It was well past his bedtime, but of course he didn't often have company to talk to.

That left the old clock tick-tocking away all to itself in the room.

Tick-tock, tick-tock.

Himself

Dan Morgan worked all alone on his farm so he talked to Himself as he dug in the fields.

"We're best by ourselves," Dan told Himself.

"Maybe we are," said Himself.

One day, down Dan's lane, came a pretty young girl, stepping light as a bird; her name was Chrissy. She looked at Dan and she liked what she saw: a sturdy young man who had fields of his own that he worked all alone.

"Speak to her, man, if you must!" said Himself. "Get her out of your head, so we can get on with our work."

"Good morning, young lady!" said Dan, very bravely.

Chrissy was too shy to speak, although she felt pleased that Dan called her a lady. She blushed red and walked on.

"I spoke, and she didn't, and that leaves me looking a fool!" Dan told Himself. "She's too fine a lady to speak to a man that works rough in the fields."

"You could spruce yourself up," suggested Himself. "Put a rose in your hat and you'll be a new Dan."

"That's all very well," Dan told Himself. "But what about you?"

"I'll stay where I am, hidden inside you, where she can't see," said Himself.

The next day Dan went to the fair with a rose in his hat and Chrissy was there in her Sunday-best clothes, so she'd look like a lady for Dan. They met and they stopped for a chat, and this led to that, greatly delighting them both. Chrissy rode home in the cart with her father, to save her fine shoes, which she held on her lap. She had only the one pair, so she needed to save them for being with Dan.

And so it went on as you'd guess. No work was done in Dan's fields, but the young couple met every day, and they talked and they walked, and Dan took her dancing at Breen's. That night his Chrissy gave him a kiss, and the kiss set poor Dan in a whirl.

"Am I sick in the head?" Dan asked Himself.

"I was thinking the same thing myself," said Himself. "But there's no help for it the way you are now. Leave the weeds to get on with growing, for it's time that you asked for her hand!"

That shook Dan to the roots of his boots.

"She'd never have me," Dan told Himself.

"She'll never have you if you don't ask!" said Himself. "What I think is this: she's seen the new Dan and she likes him. If he asks her, she'll have him, so long as she doesn't see me."

"And what will we do about you?" Dan asked Himself.

"I'll stay hidden inside the new Dan," said Himself. "You don't need the rough honest man when you're doing your wooing. Save that man for the work in the fields."

"I'll give it a go," Dan told Himself and he put on his suit and went off to speak to her father. When Dan came back he was glowing for he had his bride promised, and three good fields of land that went with her.

Well, they were married, and Chrissy came to the farm, to live there with Dan and Himself.

"She'll want changes made," Dan told Himself. "This house is no place for a lady like Chrissy!"

"Maybe the place needed changing!" Himself replied. "Get on and do it, never mind about me!"

"Just you stay inside, and I'll do it," said Dan.

Dan set about changing the place the very first day Chrissy was there. He bought her a fine settle chair that was fit for a lady to sit on, and a vase full of flowers she could look at.

"I'll do my turn in the fields," Chrissy told Dan, and she rolled up her sleeves, and took hold of the spade. She was a strong girl and she knew she should work with her man, like any girl would when she married a farmer.

"My wife should sit by the fire," replied Dan, and he took the spade from her and he sent her inside, for he knew that he'd married a pretty young girl and he thought she'd expect him to spoil her.

Chrissy had nothing to do but look at the flowers in the vase, and she soon tired of that, so she thought she'd chop wood and tell Dan the fairies had done it.

Dan caught her out on her way to the yard with the hatchet.

"That's no job for a lady like you," Dan scolded Chrissy. "You leave that alone, Chrissy dear. You sit in my house and look pretty!" And he sent Chrissy back to her seat by the fire.

"I did that right," Dan told Himself.

"What about chopping the wood?" said Himself, but Dan didn't listen. He was too busy planning how he'd please his Chrissy to think about work that had to be done.

"It's time I got out," muttered Himself, who was afraid he might smother and die inside Dan.

"You'll stay where you are!" replied Dan. "I don't want her to see you."

Chrissy sat by the fire and thought of the Dan that she'd seen in the field the very first day that she passed. Somehow the Dan that she'd married was different.

She twiddled her thumbs and got bored. She loved Dan and wanted to please him, but how could she be the lady Dan wanted for all of the rest of her life?

She thought she'd nip up and see to the pigs.

Dan caught her at it, of course.

"I married a lady and that's what you'll be!" Dan shouted at Chrissy, and he ordered her back to the house.

That made Chrissy cross, but Dan wouldn't listen.
He stormed out of the house, and left Chrissy to weep by
the fire.

"You're to blame," Dan told Himself. "It takes a rough man
from the field to bring a lady to tears, and you've popped out
of me and you've done it!"

"And who am I but you?" grumbled Himself.

"I've changed," said Dan. "A man has to change when he
marries a lady."

"I don't know how to change," said Himself, and he twisted
and turned inside Dan, trying hard to get out, though Dan
wouldn't let him.

It was too much for Dan. Dan knew that Himself couldn't
change, deep inside, so Dan made a plan to be rid of Himself.

He rented a stone house on the far side of the hill. That way he could do the rough work in his fields with Himself without being seen by his wife.

"Don't tell a soul about the new house," Dan warned Chrissy, for he didn't want word to get round to Himself. He thought he could slip off to the new house without Himself knowing.

That night they put all their things in the cart and went off in the dark like two mice on the flit. Of course, it thundered and poured as they went the long road.

"We'll start a new life," Dan told his wife as they huddled together on top of the cart. "I'll be the man with the rose in his hat, and you'll be the fine lady I married."

"Well, maybe," Chrissy said, biting her lip. She was scared he would guess that she wasn't a lady, for she loved her Dan and she wanted to please him.

By midnight they were at the new house built of stone, wet through and shivering, but glad in their hearts, for they were young and in love and just married.

Dan opened the door with the new key, pleased as punch to be in a new house that he'd share with his wife.

He opened the door with the new key and . . .

There was Himself by the fire.

"What took you so long on the road?" said Himself.

Dan gave a roar.

Chrissy heard him shout and she thought Dan was killed so she ran into the house through the door and . . .

And there was her Dan . . . kicking Himself around the room.

AND . . .

Chrissy saw Himself, for the very first time.

"Stop kicking that man this minute!" said Chrissy to Dan.

Himself was all mud from the work in the fields but Chrissy thought he was nice, and he had a look of her Dan, although he had no rose in his hat.

The more she looked at Himself, the more she saw Dan!

"Who is this poor man?" she asked Dan. "Who is this poor man you've been kicking?"

"Well . . . Himself is myself, the way I really am," confessed Dan, blushing red. "I've tried to get rid of Himself, for he's just a rough man that works in the fields and not good enough to be married to you."

"Now I see how it is," Chrissy said with a smile. "But wait till I show you my secret!" and she opened the door and called to someone she'd left crying there, out in the cold.

"Here's someone just like Himself," she told Dan. "Someone I've kept hidden from you."

And in from the dark walked . . .

Herself.

And then something strange happened.

There were four in the room but . . . the four became two . . .

Dan and Chrissy.

The Hunger

In the time of the Hunger when the people were cast on the roads starving, the young Lady Charles came home to her fine house, the bride of Lord Charles.

They rode through the gates in their carriage, and the Hunger was there, but my Lady Charles paid no heed, for she was a lady, and didn't she know it! She could eat her fill whenever she fancied, so why would she care for the Hunger?

Lord Charles was past sixty and gouty; my lady was just seventeen, and as plump in the breast as a pheasant. They were well matched, after the fashion of lords and their ladies . . . ill-matched, some would say, but no one said that to Lord Charles, or his lady.

Next day she sat out on the lawn, eating fresh salmon and dill and cream cheese.

Says she to Lord Charles, "My dear, now I'm here, we must throw a fine ball for the County, the night of the races."

"It might not look well, when the Hunger is there, at the gate," says Lord Charles, making short work of a grape that she'd placed in his mouth.

"Never mind that," says my lady, licking her pretty fingers. "Let them work for their food, like you do, my dear." And she gave him a look full of sweetness, that banished his care for the Hunger.

"Well, we will, my dear heart," sighed Lord Charles, who could never resist his young lady.

Lady Charles clapped her hands in delight, and she gave her old husband a peck on his cheek that just might have passed for a kiss. Then she went back to her eating. She'd no thought for the Hunger, for she'd eaten good food all her life.

On the night of the ball, all the Quality came. The rooms were lit up from one tower to the other, and carriages drew up at the door, and the rich and the fancy climbed out. They bowed and they laughed and they chattered, passing inside to greet their old friend Lord Charles and meet his new lady.

It was "My dear Lady Charles" and "My good Lady Charles" and "To be sure, Lady Charles" and to be sure Lady Charles cut some dash, young and plump, in her silk and her rings and fine pearls and the gold thread she ran through her hair. My young Lady Charles swirled in the dancing with the fine men who'd come down from Town. The music was grand, and so was the food. Lord Charles was doing his bride proud, and all of the guests ate their fill.

No one mentioned the Hunger outside, at the gate.

Well, they drank and they ate and they danced and they drank and they ate and they danced and they drank and they ate a bit more, and they chattered and chattered and chattered away as the warm night grew on, and the moon rose high up over the house.

Then . . . my Lady Charles slipped out into her garden, alone, and ran down to the walk by the lake.

I've heard people say that she'd someone to meet by the lake, some young man who'd swirled her around in the dance, and whispered soft words in her ear, a young man she'd known for some time before she met and married Lord Charles. Her footsteps were light and her young heart was filled up with the song and the dance, and the wine that was in her which added a flavour to savour, and made her eyes brighten the night.

There she was, in the night, by the lilies that grew at the edge of the lake, waiting for her young man to come, so they say, while old Lord Charles

looked about his fine rooms, wondering where was the sweet
flower that he'd brought to his house, to brighten his life.

And the Hunger was there by the lake, with starvation
in its eyes.

It came to her in the dark.

It plucked at her skirt and begged her for food.

"We've no food to spare!" says my lady, turning her heel,
and a fine heel it was, beneath her young flesh.

"Eat the grass!" says my lady, all puffed up with rage,
so her white flesh glowed red on her face.

"But be sure it's your own grass you eat and not ours!" says my Lady Charles, and wasn't her hot young flesh enticing?

And she struck it a blow on the cheek and thrust it aside as she turned away. What happened next no one knows, for no one else was there, save my Lady Charles all stuffed up with wine and fine tasty food, and one who was all skin and thin bone and begged her for some morsel to put in its belly, yearning and gurning for food.

"Where's my young wife?" says Lord Charles, as he laid down his glass.

"No doubt she's gone out for some air," said one of his friends, with a wink to the others. They all knew what she was about, but no one said that to Lord Charles. They were full of his wine, and no one would risk it.

"My wife should be here to see to her guests," grumbled Lord Charles. And he sent for the servants and told them to find his young wife.

They didn't look too hard at first. They had a good mind where they'd find the young lady, and some thought she'd best be left where she was with her folly . . . but no one said that to Lord Charles.

Time passed, and my lord grew impatient. He stamped and he swore and he heaved himself out of the chair, and he went to look for his wife, with some of the guests, though not many bothered to search carefully. They'd seen the plump girl dance with the light in her eye, and they'd seen the look of the young men that waltzed her. They knew Lord Charles had married a wife who could stray, but no one said that to Lord Charles.

"She's gone!" swore Lord Charles. "Bad cess to her for I married a cheat of a girl who's run off with some man!"

That's what his world knows of the fate of the young Lady Charles, for that is the story his friends put about when they laughed at Lord Charles in their cups, but . . .

There's a tale round the town of a huddle of a thing that was gnawed and left rotting red-raw in the wood, and fine hair threaded with gold that was caught on a thorn, and a bundle of clothes drenched in blood, hidden under a stone by the edge of the lake. And wasn't she plump, and wasn't she proud, and wasn't she stuffed like a pheasant and laced with good wine, a feast that would tempt a poor thing that was starved, and had nothing to eat?

They're saying my lady got served what she deserved . . . and maybe she did.

They're saying my lady got ate by Hunger. That's how the tale goes . . . but no one's said *that* to Lord Charles.

Little Bridget

Bridget O'Flynn was a wild little child who liked playing about in the field. "Don't be alone in the field or the fairies will get you!" her mother told her. But Bridget had no fear of the fairies, for they'd never caught her before, though she often played in the field when her brothers and sisters were out.

One day Bridget stayed in the field far too long, and dusk came, and Bridget was cold coming home and her legs had an ache from her running about, and she caught a stone in her shoe.

She sat down and took her shoe off, and shook out the stone.

Then she heard a small sound, like the music that's made by a river, although there was no river there.

She sat still and listened, and somehow the soft music sent her to sleep.

Maybe she dreamt that she heard a strange singing and dancing and laughing and larking about, and maybe she went to see what it was that was making such a noise in her field. Maybe she did and maybe she didn't. It may be that she wasn't dreaming

at all, but awake in her sleep and bewitched. Maybe she saw some Little Things in the corn, and some more Little Things dancing and prancing all around her, moving about, and some of the Little Things called her by name.

"Bridget O'Flynn! You're wanted below!"

"Bridget O'Flynn! Follow us in!"

"Bridget O'Flynn! You'll not have us waiting for you!"

Maybe she followed them down the field to a hole in the ground that she'd not seen before, there by the thorn tree. Maybe there was no hole in the ground. Maybe it never was there.

Maybe she went in.

She never came home to her father and mother, Phelim and Mary O'Flynn.

The family searched high and low, high and low, Phelim and Mary O'Flynn, and her sisters and brothers, Anna and Seamus, Maureen and Joe, John Paul and Patrick. All of the neighbours came out and helped in the search for the little O'Flynn that was lost in the field: McCann the milkman, and the family O'Boyle who had the top field, and the Meehans from over the brae, and McGraw from Glenowen. They all were out looking for Bridget O'Flynn, that maybe the fairies had stolen away.

All they found was one yellow shoe that Bridget had left where she stopped to take out the stone that was bothering her foot. She left the yellow shoe there on the ground, never knowing she'd left it behind her.

They thought Little Bridget was dead and they grieved after her.

They kept her place by the fire for a long time, just in case she'd come home, but she didn't.

Little Bridget was gone and almost forgotten, though they had a Mass said on her saint's day.

The years passed away and so did her father and mother, Phelim and Mary O'Flynn. They are buried below in Ramore. Her sisters and brothers died too, one by one. Seamus passed on with the fever and Maureen was too good to live, so she died, when she wasn't much older than Bridget. Joe lived to be old, but he died as well, and John Paul and Patrick were lost in the war.

Bridget's whole family were dead, except for Anna, who wed and had sons and a daughter who all but one upped and left her and went to the States. One stayed on the farm. That was young Phelim. One son was all the small farm could keep.

After her husband had died and passed on, Anna worked on the farm with young Phelim. They did very well, for they worked very hard to look after the land that looked after them. They sold their crops and their cattle, and they bought up more land in the years that were good.

Threescore years and more passed Anna by, till she grew old
and weak and sat by the fire with her stick, for she couldn't work
any more. Her son, the young Phelim, aged fifty, was running the
farm, and a fine farm it was, for he had the land that belonged to
the O'Boyles, and the land of the Meehans, and the bog lake forbye
that used to belong to McGraw. The old neighbours were gone to
the grave, and their children had moved to the city for work.

Only Anna was left from the old times, biding her time by the
fire, and she hadn't the strength in her legs to go out of the house,
or the power in her eyes to see to the tip of her nose.

It was late one night, and Anna sat crouched by the fire, a
slave to rheumatism and gout.

There was a knock at the door, but Anna was too old to
answer, and Phelim was over the way helping out at the house
of the priest, Father O'Rawe.

The door opened wide, and in came a small child with one
shoe on its foot, the other foot bare.

The child came up to Anna, face on, and she said: "Who are
you? Why are you here in our house?" just like that.

Now Anna, half blind, couldn't see much of the child, just a blur, but she prodded the child with the tip of her stick, in case it would step on her foot that was sore with the gout.

"Why are you here in our house?" asked the child, sounding scared.

"Whose house do you think you're in?" answered Anna, quite sharp, although something stirred in her that bothered her mind. Maybe it was the voice of the child, for somehow she thought she knew it.

"Our house, O'Flynn's!" cried the child. "Where is my mammy?"

"Your mammy?" said Anna. "There's no mammy here!"

"And where is my daddy and sisters and brothers?" the child said, with tears in her voice.

"Hush, child, don't cry," said Anna.

The child wouldn't be hushed.

She turned right around, looking at all the new things in the room.

"Where's our mammy's chair and the clock on the wall, and who is that man coming in by our door?"

It was Phelim who'd come in through the door.

He looked at the strange child, with one shoe, and he didn't know her from Eve.

He thought she was a gypsy come from the field, to rob or to steal from his mother.

"Have you no home to go to? Get out of this house!" said Phelim. "And don't you be teasing my old wheezy mother!"

The child fled from the house.

The Haunting at Soft Butter's Farm

There once was an old farmer called Butter. He was gentle and kind and lived all by himself with a pig and a sheep and a goat that he spoiled, for he loved them too much, which is no way for a farmer to be.

"Pigs are for killing for bacon, and sheep are for shearing, and we get fine cheese from our goat!" people told him.

"Is that so?" said the farmer, and he moved the pig and the sheep and the goat into the house with himself, for they were his friends.

Everyone thought he was mad. They called him 'Soft Butter'. I don't think he was mad. I think he was lonely.

One day Soft Butter went to the fair, and he met a fine girl called Miranda. She hadn't a penny to put to her name, but she had a good heart, and she fell for Soft Butter. She made him feel grand with her hand on his arm. She soon had Soft Butter bewitched with her smile, though that doesn't take much with a lonely old man.

"Will you wed?" asked Soft Butter.

"Have you a pig?" asked Miranda.

"I have," said Soft Butter.

"Have you a sheep?" asked Miranda.

"I have," said Soft Butter.

"Have you a goat?" asked Miranda.

"I have," said Soft Butter, a little surprised that she'd asked, for he thought she would follow her heart, and he knew it was good.

"Then I'll wed!" said Miranda, quite quickly in case he'd think of changing his mind.

It wasn't a trick or a scheme. She loved him. She wanted to marry Soft Butter, but she'd been told what to ask by her Aunt Clicky Tongue, and she was afraid of her auntie.

And so they were married the next market-day and Miranda went out to the farm with Soft Butter.

She made good friends with the pig and the sheep and the goat, for she was gentle and kind like Soft Butter. The pair were well met.

That should have been that, but it wasn't.

The week after they wed, with her hat on her head and her bag in her hand, up the lane to the farm came Aunt Clicky Tongue. She marched in through the door on the two love-a-doves, without even asking their leave.

"Here's a fine house!" said Aunt Clicky Tongue. "But the beasts would keep better out in the field!"

And she turfed out the pig and the sheep and the goat.

"Now see here . . ." began old Soft Butter.

"See what?" said Aunt Clicky Tongue. "See what-did-you-say?" And she gave him a look that would kill.

"Oh, never mind," said Soft Butter, turning away, for he couldn't stand up to Aunt Clicky Tongue. He was too kind and too gentle to cross her.

"There's room here for more!" said Aunt Clicky Tongue, and she sent for her cousin, old Joe, and her three spotty sisters, and two friends and their uncle with pains in his knee.

They all came up the lane to Soft Butter's Farm, and Soft Butter went down to the road and brought up their bags, for Aunt Clicky Tongue told him to do it.

"There's no room for us all!" mumbled Soft Butter.

"Then you may sleep in the barn!" said Aunt Clicky Tongue. "For these are your guests in your house, and you cannot be putting them out!"

"Aunty dear . . ." murmured Miranda.

"What's this? Have you something to say?" growled Aunt Clicky Tongue.

"I said nothing at all," said Miranda, just wilting away, for she was very scared of her auntie.

The two lovey-doves set up their nest in the barn, and the house was filled with the aunt and her people. Aunt Clicky Tongue charged some of them rent, which she kept for herself so it wouldn't bother Miranda.

None of them worked, except Soft Butter and Soft Butter's wife.

It was "Butter, do this!" and "Butter, do that!" and "Butter, don't be forgetting to do things our way!" all the day from Aunt Clicky Tongue, her cousin, old Joe, her three sisters, the two friends and their uncle with pains in his knee.

It all got too much for Soft Butter. He sat in the field with the pig and the sheep and the goat and he sighed, but that didn't do him much good.

He gave up, and he died in the field with his friends.

Poor Miranda! She cried and she sobbed her heart out for Soft Butter.

"No more of that, girl!" said her Aunt Clicky Tongue. "The old man was soft! We're much better without him."

They buried Soft Butter in the low field, for Aunt Clicky Tongue wouldn't let Miranda pay gold for a grave at the church. She told Miranda they needed their money to pay for the living.

It was a mistake, though she didn't know it, for somehow Soft Butter was still on the farm, just waiting for something to waken his heart.

Now there was no one to do any work round the place but Miranda. She did what she was bid by her Aunt Clicky Tongue, slaving all day to care for the rest but, oh dear! she was missing Soft Butter.

The poor girl hid in the low field by the grave and she grieved for Soft Butter, with the pig and the sheep and the goat, who were sorely put out. No one else knew she was sad, and no one else cared.

But something stirred in the field, wakened by the tears that the girl shed for Soft Butter.

The very next night, with the daylight growing dim, there was a stir in the yard. The two friends and their uncle with pains in the knee all ran to look, though the uncle ran slowly because of his pains.

There was a ghost in the yard, white as a sheet and gliding about. There was no moaning and groaning or clanging of chains, for he wasn't that kind of ghost.

"A g-g-ghost!" cried the uncle with pains.

"Never mind that," said the pig, looking over the fence. "Sure, it's only the ghost of our friend the farmer, Soft Butter!"

But the two friends and the uncle with pains paid no heed to a pig (even a pig who could talk), for they knew a ghost when they saw one. They thought it would eat them alive!

"AHHHHHHHHH!" screamed the two friends and the uncle with pains in his knee. They were scared stiff by the ghost-in-the-yard and they ran off over the fields in their nightclothes. The uncle ran fastest of all getting out, and jumped highest of all getting over the gate, so it seems he was cured of the pains in his knee.

They never came back to Soft Butter's Farm. Nobody minded, and nobody missed them, though Aunt Clicky Tongue thought she would miss the rent.

The next night was worse! There was the ghost in the front room where the three spotty sisters slept on the floor, and old Cousin Joe had the sofa. The ghost hovered about above them and wakened them up. It was gentle and kind and would do them no harm, but they didn't know that. They were frightened.

"Never mind that!" said the sheep, looking in at the window. "It's only the ghost of our friend the farmer, Soft Butter."

The three spotty sisters and old Cousin Joe paid no heed to the sheep, for they didn't believe that they had heard a sheep talking, but they knew very well that they'd seen a ghost . . .

They fled out of the house, down the lane, screaming their heads off. They never came back to Soft Butter's Farm. Nobody minded, and nobody missed them, for they were Family and didn't pay rent to Aunt Clicky Tongue.

Next night came, and there was the ghost in Aunt Clicky Tongue's room.

Something was drifting about by the bed, over her head. It was too much for Aunt Clicky Tongue! She stuck her hat on her head, and belted right out of the house down the lane.

The goat watched her go, but he didn't say anything. He was a wise goat for a goat, and he wanted her out of the way! So he didn't say it was only the ghost of his friend the farmer, Soft Butter, in case she believed him and stayed.

Aunt Clicky Tongue never came back to Soft Butter's farm, not even to pick up her teeth which she'd left in the glass, nor the rent money she'd kept from Miranda.

The loss of the teeth put an end to their clicking, and the loss of the money just served her right!

The last night of all there was no one to scare, for no one was there but Miranda, and Soft Butter's ghost . . . there in the glow by the fire, with the pig and the sheep and the wise goat, fetched in from the field. They were together again for a while. It was a gentle sweet time for them all, being together again. Then Soft Butter's ghost faded away in the firelight, at home, with his friends, and that was the end of Soft Butter.

But it wasn't the end of Miranda. She stayed on the farm, with the pig and the sheep and the goat. The love in their hearts for Soft Butter helped her to live out her life. When she died she was buried right there in the low field, beside her Soft Butter . . . And so were the pig and the sheep and the goat when they died in their turn.

They're all ghosts now, out in the field, Soft Butter, Miranda, the pig and the sheep and the goat. They're still there together haunting the field, the ghosts of Soft Butter, Miranda, the pig and the sheep and the goat.

More about the Stories

Boneless and the Tinker

It's a lonely old Boneless, is Boneless. Neither male nor female, Boneless is a kind of house spirit, attached to a deserted old farm, remote and lonely. I had a particular remote and ruined farmhouse in mind when I wrote this. I was up there the other day. It has now been turned into a silage store with a slurry pit. If there is a Boneless there, I don't think It would be too pleased . . . though what It might do to the slurry and the farmer who has misused Its place might be entertaining.

Death and the Neighbours at Ness

This one is a bad case of graveyard disturbance, leading to a ghastly version of a knock-knock joke, with unfresh corpses calling at old Nagger's farm to complain to her grandson Fintan McGlone. All this coming and going gives Death problems. 'Doing a deal with Death' stories are common enough in Ireland, and I felt I had to have one in the collection, but I didn't realise how much fun I was going to have writing it.

Gallows Hill

The county town near me, Downpatrick, has its own Gallows Hill up beyond Saul Street. Only the name remains, but it is a reminder of what used to be, when corpses were hung out as warning to the peasantry. I took that idea, and the idea of the drunkard's excuse when he comes home from the fair with no money, and tied them together with the tale of Jackie Golightly's donkey that wants to go home with his master. The problem is, Jackie Golightly's been hanged, and the corpse has got just a bit into decay . . .

The Ghostly Penny

Near where I live is a cold, grey lough called Lough Island Reavy. It is a stark, exposed stretch of water in a barren lowland place, with mountains rising from it. There are stone walls and whins and one or two little cottages and the traces of Hunger fields and an ancient underground souterrain. I was scared of the lough as a child, and I am none too comfy there as an adult. This story came from the strange feeling of that place, though somewhere along the way the lough itself got lost. I wanted to write about the remoteness of the existence of the people who lived there when I was a child, and the way a grudge could linger down the decades. It is a story about clinging on to life, in more ways than one . . .

Himself

I wrote this story partly with the Irish storyteller Liz Weir in mind. I was thinking how she would enjoy the teasing play with the word "himself" and the mischief of the whole thing. It felt great to be able to do a story that was at once light and funny, but at the same time had a very serious edge to it. Like Dan, we all put roses in our hats and present the outside world with what we hope is an acceptable pattern of behaviour, but what happens if this puts us at odds with the feelings of the real Dan inside?

The Hunger

This short raw story wrote itself, though it was finished a long time after the others. That many (though not by any means all) of the big landowners enjoyed life to the full while the people were starving in the fields and lanes around their big houses is not in dispute, though I doubt if any of them met with the fate which awaits Lady Charles . . . but didn't she deserve it, just! I thought I could be allowed at least one really nasty ending, and this is it.

Little Bridget

There are plenty of versions of the old country story of the child-taken-by-the-fairies, but I wanted to concentrate on the confusion and terror and sadness of the child when she returns to her home, unaware that what would have been her lifetime has passed by while she strayed in the timeless world of the fairies. That is what I have tried to do with Bridget O'Flynn in this story, in the hope that readers will feel her sadness, and the sense of her removal from her own familiar world.

The Haunting at Soft Butter's Farm

Many a big man is meek and mild and accommodating in his soul, and lets the world run rings round him. In Ireland we would call such a man "soft as butter", and it was this phrase that led me to write this story of a gentle ghost. The names in the story are part of the game: Aunt Clicky Tongue and Soft Butter and the lovely Miranda. I would have to admit that I haven't met many Irish country girls called Miranda, but the name seemed right, and it is my story so I used it.